For Wally

Second U.S. edition 1997

Library of Congress Cataloging-in-Publication Data is available.

ISBN 0-7636-0310-4

2 4 6 8 10 9 7 5 3 1

Printed in Hong Kong

This book was typeset in Wallyfont.
The pictures were done in watercolor and water based ink.

Candlewick Press
2067 Massachusetts Avenue
Cambridge, Massachusetts 02140

MARTIN HANDFORD

CANDLEWICK PRESS
CAMBRIDGE, MASSACHUSETTS

HI, FRIENDS!

MY NAME IS WALDO. I'M JUST SETTING OFF ON A WORLDWIDE HIKE. YOU CAN COME TOO. ALL YOU HAVE TO DO IS FIND ME.

I'VE GOT ALL I NEED — WALKING STICK, KETTLE, MALLET, CUP, BACKPACK, SLEEPING BAG, BINOCULARS, CAMERA, SNORKEL, BELT, BAG, AND SHOVEL.

BY THE WAY, I'M NOT TRAVELING ON MY OWN. WHEREVER I GO, THERE ARE LOTS OF OTHER CHARACTERS FOR YOU TO SPOT. FIRST FIND WOOF (BUT ALL YOU CAN SEE IS HIS TAIL), WENDA, WIZARD WHITEBEARD, AND ODLAW. THERE ARE ALSO 25 WALDO-WATCHERS SOMEWHERE, EACH OF WHOM APPEARS ONLY ONCE IN MY TRAVELS. CAN YOU FIND ONE OTHER CHARACTER WHO APPEARS IN EVERY SCENE? ALSO IN EVERY SCENE, CAN YOU SPOT MY KEY, WOOF'S BONE, WENDA'S CAMERA, WIZARD WHITEBEARD'S SCROLL, AND ODLAW'S BINOCULARS?

WOW! WHAT A SEARCH! Waldo

GREETINGS,
WALDO-FOLLOWERS!
WOW, THE BEACH WAS
GREAT TODAY! I SAW
THIS GIRL STICK AN
ICE-CREAM CONE IN HER
BROTHER'S FACE, AND
THERE WAS A SAND-
CASTLE WITH A REAL
KNIGHT IN ARMOR
INSIDE! FANTASTIC!

Waldo

WHERE'S
AT THE BEACH
WALDO?

TO:
WALDO-FOLLOWERS
HERE, THERE,
EVERYWHERE

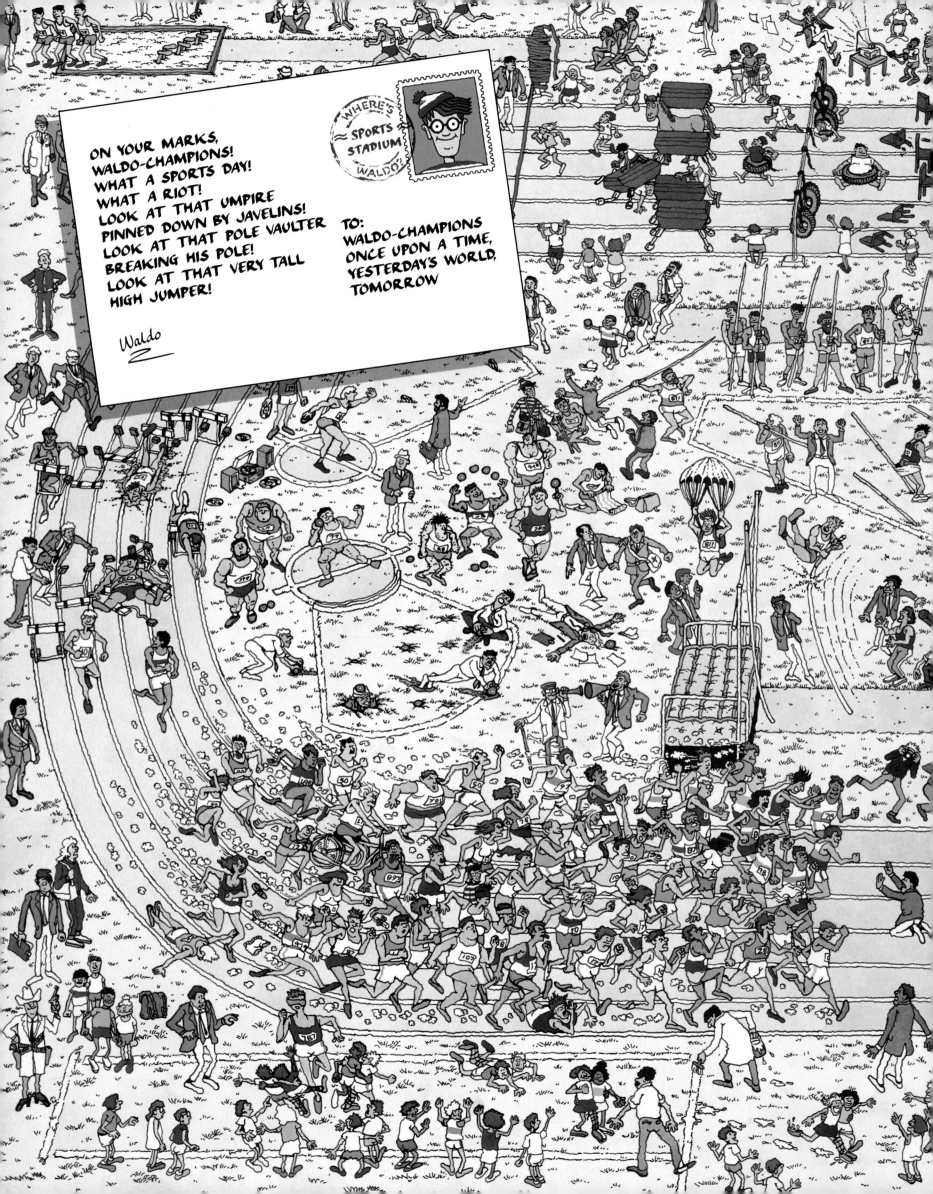

STEP RIGHT UP, WALDO-FUN LOVERS! WOW! I'VE LOST ALL MY THINGS, ONE IN EVERY PLACE. NOW YOU HAVE TO GO BACK AND FIND THEM. AND SOMEWHERE ONE OF THE WALDO-WATCHERS HAS LOST THE BOBBLE FROM HIS HAT. CAN YOU SPOT WHICH ONE AND FIND THE MISSING BOBBLE?

Waldo

WHERE'S FAIRGROUND WALDO?

TO:
WALDO-FUN LOVERS
BACK TO THE BEGINNING,
START AGAIN,
TERRIFIC

THE GREAT WHERE'S WALDO? CHECKLIST
Hundreds more things for Waldo-watchers to watch out for!

IN TOWN
- A dog on a roof
- A man on a fountain
- A man about to trip over a dog's leash
- A car crash
- A happy barber
- People in a street, watching TV
- A puncture caused by a Roman arrow
- A tearful tune
- A boy attacked by a plant
- A waiter who isn't concentrating
- A robber who's been clobbered
- A face on a wall
- A man coming out of a manhole
- A man feeding pigeons
- A bicycle crash

SKI SLOPES
- A man reading on a roof
- A flying skier
- A runaway skier
- A backward skier
- A portrait in snow
- An illegal fisherman
- A snowball in the neck
- Two unconscious skiers
- Two skiers hitting trees
- An Alpine horn
- A snow skier
- A flag collector
- Two very scruffy skiers
- A skier up a tree
- A water-skier on snow
- An abominable snowman
- A skiing reindeer
- A roof jumper
- A heap of skaters

THE TRAIN STATION
- A boy falling from a train
- A breakdown on tracks
- Naughty children on a train roof
- People being knocked over by a door
- A man about to step on a ball
- Three different times at the same time
- A wheelbarrow baby carriage
- A face on a train
- Five people reading one newspaper
- A struggling bag carrier
- A showoff with suitcases
- A man losing everything from his cases
- A smoking train
- A squeeze on a bench
- A dog tearing a man's trousers
- Fare dodgers
- A hand caught between doors
- A cattle stampede
- A man breaking a weighing machine

ON THE BEACH
- A dog biting a boy's bottom
- A man who is overdressed
- A muscular man with a medal
- A popular girl
- A water-skier on water
- A striped photo
- A punctured air mattress
- A donkey who likes ice cream
- A man being squashed
- A punctured beach ball
- A human pyramid
- A human steppingstone
- Two odd friends
- A cowboy
- A human donkey
- Age and beauty
- A boy who follows in his father's footsteps
- Two men with vests, one without
- A boy being tortured by a spider
- A showoff with sandcastles
- A gang of hat robbers
- An Arab making pyramids
- Three protruding tongues
- Two oddly fitting hats
- An odd couple
- Five spiders
- A towel with a hole in it
- A punctured pontoon boat
- A boy who's not allowed any ice cream

CAMPSITE
- A bull in a hedge
- Bull horns
- A shark in a canal
- A bull seeing red
- A careless kick
- Tea in a lap
- A low bridge
- People knocked over by a mallet
- A man surprised undressing
- A bicycle tire about to be punctured
- Camper's camels
- A scarecrow that doesn't work
- A wigwam
- Large biceps
- A collapsed tent
- A smoking barbecue
- A fisherman catching old boots
- An old-fashioned bicycle
- Boy Scouts making fire
- A roller-skating hiker
- A man blowing up a boat
- A camper's butler
- Runners on a road
- A bull chasing children
- Scruffy campers
- Thirsty walkers

SPORTS STADIUM
- Three pairs of feet, sticking out of sand
- A cowboy starting races
- Hopeless hurdlers
- Ten children with fifteen legs
- A record thrower
- A shot put juggler
- An ear trumpet
- A vaulting horse
- A runner with two wheels
- A parachuting vaulter
- A Scotsman with a caber
- An elephant pulling a rope
- People being knocked over by a hammer
- A gardener
- Three frogmen
- A nude runner
- A bed
- A bandaged boy
- A runner with four legs
- A sunken jumper
- A man with an odd pair of legs
- A man chasing a dog, chasing a cat
- A boy squirting water

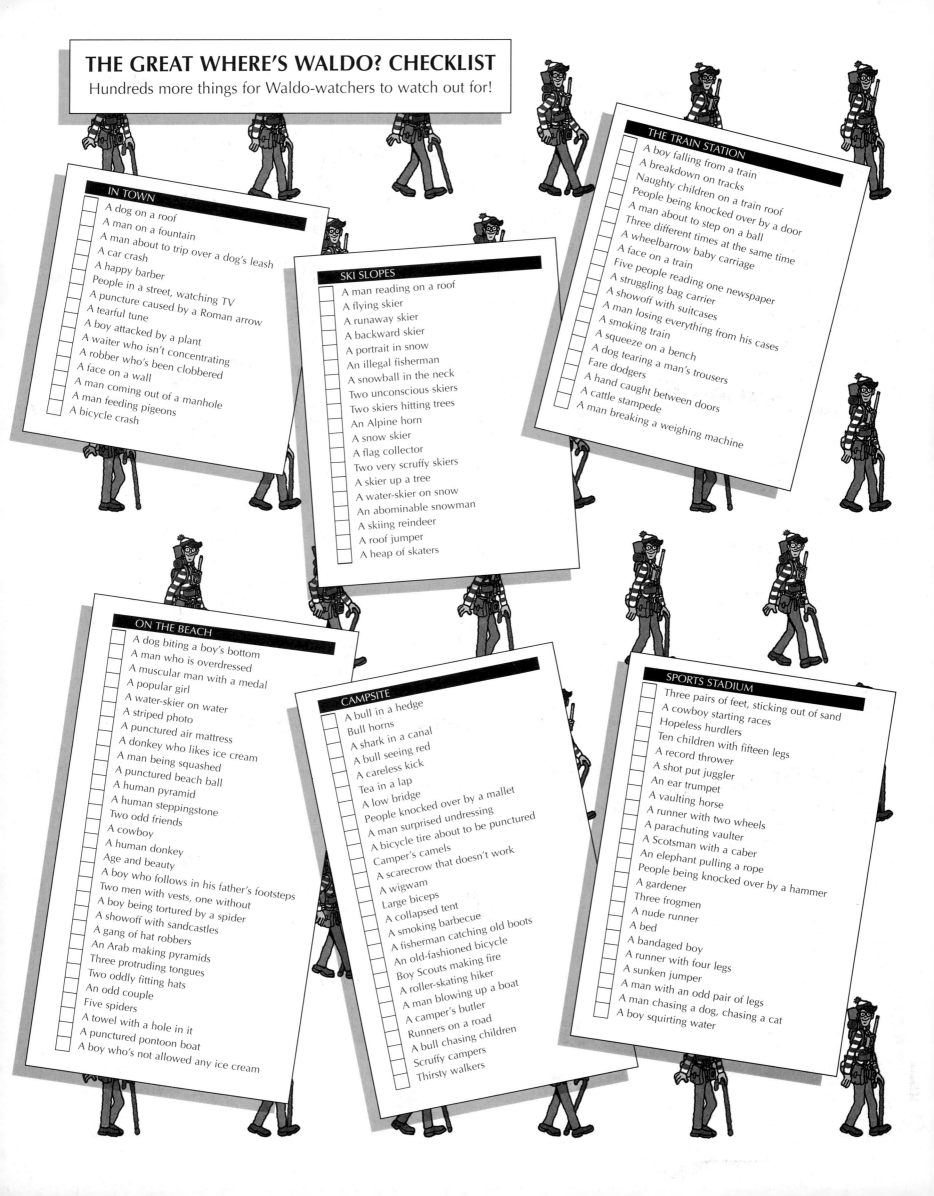